Wake up, Bear

Lynley Dodd

Gareth Stevens Publishing
Milwaukee

It was time for Bear to wake up.
He had been asleep for many months,
ALL winter, in fact.
Now it was Spring.

His friends came to his cave
under the Bulbul tree and said,
"Hi Bear, time to get up."
But he wouldn't wake up.
He just lay there,
smiling dozily,
and went right on
snoring.

Lion shook his mane and roared.
It was a rumbling, grumbling,
SCARY roar,
and it made everyone jump with fright.
But Bear went right on
snoring.

Squirrel dropped an acorn on Bear's nose.
BONK went the acorn,
but it didn't bother Bear.
He just went right on
snoring.

Monkey curled the end
of his long spidery tail
and tickled Bear's toes.
Bear twitched a little,
here and there,
but he still went right on
snoring.

Parrot brought her family,
uncles, grandmothers, and all.
They sat in the Bulbul tree
and squawked and screeched
until their throats were sore
and their beaks were stiff.
The noise was awful,
but Bear went right on
snoring.

Cat arched his back,
bristled his fur
and yowled,
"w...w...rr...OWWWWW!"
His mother could hear him a mile away,
but Bear didn't hear him at all.
He just went right on
snoring.

Elephant went down to the river
and filled her trunk with water.
She whooshed it at Bear.
SPLAT!
Bear was soaking wet,
and drips dropped off the end of his nose,
but he still went right on
snoring.

Owl sat on a twig above Bear's cave.
He took a deep breath,
until all his feathers stuck out,
and hooted,
"oo . . .ooOOOOOoo."
The smallest animals hid in the grass,
but Bear went right on
snoring.

Hippo opened her mouth
and gave an enormous yawn.
It showed every one of her teeth
and her tonsils too.
She looked TERRIBLE,
but Bear didn't see her.
He just went right on
snoring.

Goat stuck up his tail,
bent down his head,
and butted Bear.
BOOMPH!
He got Bear's fur in his nose and ears,
but Bear didn't feel a thing.
He just went right on
snoring.

Snake twined and slithered
round and down the Bulbul tree.
She hissed,
"sssssssSSSSSSssssss."
It made the animals shiver,
but not Bear.
He just kept right on
snoring.

"It's no good," said everyone sadly,
"We've roared,
bonked,
tickled,
screeched,
yowled,
whooshed,
hooted,
yawned,
butted,
and hissed ourselves silly,
and Bear WON'T wake up.
We might as well go home."

Just then a bee came buzzing past.

Z Z Z Z Z Z Z Z Z Z Z Z Z Z Z Z Z Z Z Z Z Z Z Z Z Z Z Z Z Z Z Z Z Z Z Z Z Z

went the bee around Bear's head.

"HONEY!" said Bear,
and he woke up.

By Lynley Dodd:

GOLD STAR FIRST READERS
Hairy Maclary from Donaldson's Dairy
Hairy Maclary's Bone
Hairy Maclary Scattercat
The Apple Tree
The Smallest Turtle
Wake Up, Bear

Library of Congress Cataloging in Publication Data

Dodd, Lynley.
 Wake up, bear.

 (Gold star first readers)
 Summary: Despite all their efforts none of the animals
can get bear to wake up from his winter sleep.
 [1. Bears — Fiction. 2. Animals — Fiction] I. Title.
II. Series.
PZ7.D6627Wak 1987   [E]   86-42798
ISBN 1-55532-149-6
ISBN 1-55532-124-0 (lib. bdg.)

North American edition first published in 1988 by
Gareth Stevens, Inc.
7317 West Green Tree Road
Milwaukee, Wisconsin 53223, USA